TO BOLDLY GO

*To all young readers—may you boldly go toward building
a better future for everyone.—A.D.*

For Auggie and Luka—L.S.

This book has not been approved, licensed,
or sponsored by any entity involved in the production
or distribution of *Star Trek: The Original Series*.

To Boldly Go: How Nichelle Nichols and *Star Trek* Helped
Advance Civil Rights

Text copyright © 2023 by Angela Dalton

Illustrations copyright © 2023 by Lauren Semmer

www.harpercollinschildrens.com

Library of Congress Control Number: 2022931770
ISBN 978-0-06-307321-0

The artist used Procreate and Photoshop to create
the digital illustrations for this book.

Design by Elaine Lopez-Levine

22 23 24 25 26 RTLO 10 9 8 7 6 5 4 3 2 1

❖

First Edition

TO BOLDLY GO

HOW **Nichelle Nichols** and **Star Trek**
Helped Advance Civil Rights

Written by
Angela Dalton

Illustrated by
Lauren Semmer

HARPER
An Imprint of HarperCollinsPublishers

It was TV night—the best night—and I could hear the

click- click- clicking

of buttons as Dad searched for the right channel.
As the sweet, syrupy goodness of red Kool-Aid splashed
into my glass, I knew the real treat was yet to come.

Mom, Dad, and I settled into place, and as the opening began,
I followed along out loud:

"Space: the final frontier. These are the voyages of the starship
Enterprise. Its five-year mission: to explore strange new worlds.
To seek out new life and new civilizations.

"To boldly go where no man has gone before!"

The show was *Star Trek,* and we instantly fell under the spell of watching Captain James T. Kirk and his crew make peace and live in harmony with different life-forms across the galaxy. But he wasn't the reason why we watched.

We watched to see Lieutenant Uhura perform
her duties as the starship's communications officer.

Hailing
frequencies
open, sir.

NICHELLE NICHOLS

Lieutenant Uhura was played by actress Nichelle Nichols, and we burst with pride seeing someone who looked like us standing as an equal to make the future better for everyone. This was important not just to my family but for all Black people, because our reality told a very different story.

When *Star Trek* first appeared on TV, America swirled in a whirlpool of change.

Dr. Martin Luther King Jr. and other civil rights leaders joined together to inspire people to march peacefully for equality and the rights of Black people.

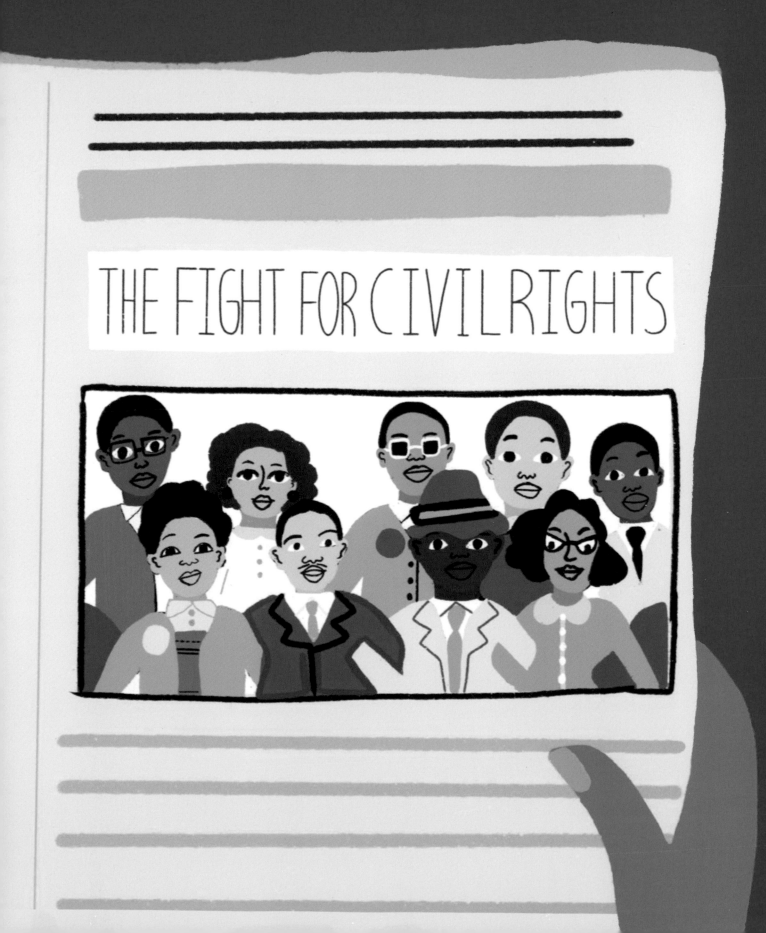

THE FIGHT FOR CIVIL RIGHTS

After *Star Trek* showed the possibilities of peace among life-forms during prime-time hours, the nightly news showed the real-life suffering the marchers endured because of racism.

Attack dogs.

Fire hoses.

Jail.

People watched as this happened to both children and adults, just because of the color of their skin.

Across the country in Hollywood, Nichelle was working to bring Uhura to life. In a time when Black actresses played servants on television, Nichelle had the unique opportunity to work with *Star Trek* creator Gene Roddenberry to create the character Uhura.

Nichelle worked on Uhura's backstory, explaining how she became a communications officer leading a team of specialists to solve difficult problems.

HISTORY of AFRICAN CULTURE

SWAHILI DICTIONARY

AFRICAN ART

Nichelle also helped discover Uhura's name; it was derived from the word *uhuru*, which means "freedom" in Swahili. For Nichelle, Uhura represented how she saw herself: strong, independent, equal.

Even as a little girl, Nichelle was confident. Her parents had taught Nichelle and her siblings that they could become whatever they wanted—and nobody could tell them otherwise.

Growing up in a home filled with music, books, and a love for art, Nichelle knew at five years old what she would grow up to be: a performer.

But at age seven, Nichelle became very ill and spent a month in the hospital. When she finally began to recover, Nichelle's doctor told her she needed exercise to regain her strength. Her parents enrolled her in ballet, and she fell in love with it, quickly proving to everyone she was a natural talent.

But, even with her talent, she was still reminded that racist people would always try to make Black people feel like they were less than white people.

Remembering what her parents taught her made Nichelle
determined to prove that this way of thinking was wrong.

And she did.
Nichelle danced ballet for many years.

As she grew older, her love for singing, dancing, and performing brought dazzling opportunities. At sixteen, she toured with the legendary bandleader Duke Ellington.

Later, she won a small role in a movie starring many Black celebrities who became her role models and lifelong friends: Maya Angelou, Pearl Bailey, Sammy Davis Jr., Sidney Poitier, and more.

Soon, Nichelle became a rising star herself. And so, when *Star Trek* began, she felt confident that she belonged wherever her talents took her.

But Hollywood had other ideas.

Working on the studio lot, Nichelle experienced the same painful reminders from her childhood—that white people did not treat Black people as equals, no matter how talented they were.

Even the *Star Trek* character she had worked so hard to bring to life became less visible on the show.

Nichelle no longer felt strong or confident. And it seemed neither she nor her character would ever be seen as important or equal. She decided there was only one thing she could do.

Head held high, she walked into *Star Trek* producer Gene Roddenberry's office and told him she was quitting the show.

"Nichelle, please think about it," he pleaded with her.

But Nichelle was sure of her decision.

The next evening, Nichelle appeared at a fundraiser as a special guest. As her eager fans gathered around her, the event host approached her.

"Nichelle, there is someone who would like to meet you." The host explained, "He's a big fan of *Star Trek* and Uhura."

Turning around, Nichelle locked eyes with the fan.

Is this happening? she thought to herself. *Was it really him?*

Standing before her was Dr. Martin Luther King Jr.!

"Yes," he said, "I am that fan."

As Dr. King explained how *Star Trek* was the only show he and his wife allowed their children to stay up late to watch, the gravity of her decision to leave the show pulled Nichelle back to reality.

"Thank you, Dr. King," she replied, "but I plan to leave *Star Trek*."

Dr. King was shocked. "Don't you realize how important your character is?"

Nichelle's head swirled with all the reasons she had to quit the show, but she continued to listen to Dr. King.

"You have opened a door that must not be allowed to close," he said. "Don't you see that you're not just a role model for Black children? You're important for people who don't look like us. For the first time, the world sees us as we should be seen, as equals, as intelligent people."

Nichelle thought about all the Black people enduring racism every day of their lives just like she was.

Her world tilted as she realized just how important she was to the show; her presence on *Star Trek* was history in the making.

Perhaps, Nichelle thought, *Uhura is a symbol of hope, a role model.*

She knew what she needed to do.

When the *Star Trek* crew returned the next season, Lieutenant Uhura reported for duty on the starship *Enterprise*.

And like the civil rights movement, while some things slowly began to change, many things stayed the same. Her lines were still cut. Uhura's character was never fully developed the way Nichelle had imagined she could be. But she never forgot what her presence meant to the lives of the people who looked like her.

And neither did they.

For over fifty years, millions of Nichelle's fans have watched *Star Trek* and continued to dream . . .

about the places . . .
and spaces . . .
they dare to envision themselves in.

To boldly go . . .
to make the future better for everyone.

OUTER
SPACE

Beyond Star Trek

Nichelle's fight for equality and interest in space exploration didn't stop when the *Star Trek* television series ended in 1969. The idea that Black people could, and should, one day travel to space planted itself in her mind. By 1977, NASA (the National Aeronautics and Space Administration) had already sent over forty astronauts into space. Of those, twenty-four had landed on the moon. It didn't go unnoticed by Nichelle that they had all been white men.

Recognizing Nichelle's ground-breaking impact on people, NASA asked if she would help them make a positive connection with women and minoritized astronaut candidates.

Nichelle accepted, but she warned, "If I put my name and reputation on the line for NASA, and I find qualified women and minority people to apply, and a year from now I still see a [white], all-male astronaut corps, I will personally file a class-action suit against NASA."

Nichelle created a recruitment campaign to find candidates across the United States. She visited colleges and high schools. She produced a film with Apollo 12 astronaut Alan Bean to support her message that "space is for everyone." She did astronaut training and received her very own